ZACH RILEY
DOWN FOR THE COUNT

Text by Paul Hoblin
Illustrated by Andrés Martínez Ricci

Published by ABDO Publishing Company, PO Box 398166, Minneapolis, MN 55439. Copyright © 2013 by Abdo Consulting Group, Inc. International copyrights reserved in all countries. No part of this book may be reproduced in any form without written permission from the publisher. SportsZone™ is a trademark and logo of ABDO Publishing Company.

Printed in the United States of America,
North Mankato, Minnesota
052012
092012

Text by: Paul Hoblin
Illustrator: Andrés Martínez Ricci

Editor: Chrös McDougall
Series Designer: Craig Hinton

Library of Congress Cataloging-in-Publication Data
Riley, Zach.
  Down for the count / by Zach Riley ; illustrated by Andres Ricci ; text by Paul Hoblin.
    p. cm. -- (Zach Riley)
  Summary: Junior is surprised to find out he made the local traveling baseball team, but when he learns why he was chosen, he is not sure that he wants to play ball on this team, even if it is bringing him closer to his father.
  ISBN 978-1-61783-533-9
  1. Baseball stories. 2. Fathers and sons--Juvenile fiction. 3. Teamwork (Sports)--Juvenile fiction. [1. Baseball--Fiction. 2. Fathers and sons--Fiction. 3. Teamwork (Sports)--Fiction.] I. Martínez Ricci, Andrés, ill. II. Hoblin, Paul. III. Title.
  PZ7.R4572Dow 2012
  813.6--dc23
                                              2012007898

TABLE OF CONTENTS

ONE

The pitch was too high, but Junior was used to pitches being too high. In fact, he *liked* them that way.

THWACK!

The sweet part of the bat connected with the ball and sent it whizzing into the outfield.

"I don't know how you hit those ones above your eyes," the pitcher, Eddie, said to Junior. Eddie picked another ball off the grass next to him and got ready to throw it toward the plate.

"When you're my height," Junior said, "every pitch is a little high."

Junior was by far the shortest kid on his neighborhood baseball team. That's why almost everyone called him Junior. He didn't mind the nickname, either. It's what people had been calling him his whole life. Of course, most people who were called Junior were called that because they had the same first name as their dad. But that had nothing to do with why he got the nickname. His dad's name was Denis, which wasn't even close to Junior's real name: Pedro.

In fact, he and his dad were nothing alike. As far as Junior could tell, his dad didn't even like baseball. The only thing they had in common was that they were both short. If you thought of it like fast food, they were both on the junior menu.

Junior swung at the next pitch and crushed that one, too. "Who cares if you're short when you can hit like that?" Eddie said.

Junior wasn't at travel team tryouts anymore. He was at his neighborhood ball field with his friend and teammate, Eddie. Everyone called Eddie by "Swish" because his favorite sport was basketball and because he always wore wind pants—even in the summer. The pants made a swishing sound when he walked.

"I didn't hit like this at the tryouts," Junior said.

"Why not?" Swish asked. "Nervous or something?" He took another ball from the bucket.

"No, I don't think so. Just one of those days where the bat kept missing the ball."

It happened to even the best players in the big leagues, Junior knew, and unfortunately it had happened to him today. Which meant he probably didn't make the team.

"You don't seem too angry about it," Swish said.

Junior shrugged. He'd never really wanted to be on the traveling team, anyway. For one thing, the traveling team ballpark was across town, and his dad was rarely around to drive him. Why bike three miles when there was a field just down the block? Besides, all his friends lived right here in the neighborhood. They spent the summer playing pickup games against other neighborhoods.

If Junior had to make a list of favorite things to do, playing these pickup games would probably be at the very top.

No, Junior didn't try out because he wanted to make the traveling team. He tried out because he wanted to see if he was good enough to make it. And now he knew the answer was yes, he was good enough.

Most days.

Just not today. Today he would have whiffed at a watermelon.

"Hold up," Swish said. He was standing on the pitching rubber again. "If tryouts are over, why did you drag me away from the basketball court to throw you batting practice?"

"I wanted to get my swing right before our first game."

"That's still like a week away."

"Exactly," Junior said. "It's only a week away."

Junior got in his batting stance. He liked to wait for the pitch with his legs almost completely straight. If he crouched as much as most batters did, the opposing pitcher had a tough time throwing the ball low enough for him to hit it.

Even standing straight up, the next pitch arrived head high. Junior slashed his bat at it.

CRACK!

The two of them watched the ball soar through the air.

"No offense, but I'm glad you didn't play well at tryouts," Swish said. "I want you on *my* team instead."

Junior looked at the ball rolling through the outfield. Just for the heck of it, he started running the bases. He rounded first and headed for second. He couldn't wait to run the bases for real, in a game. And not just any bases, either. These bases.

When he reached home plate, he breathed hard and imagined he could hear fans clapping for him, cheering him on. Not that he needed fans—it was enough just getting to stand at home plate, with or

without any added noise. He would never say it out loud because he didn't want to sound corny, but he thought *home plate* was the perfect name.

Because it was here, on this field, at this base, that he often felt most at home.

///////

When Junior got to his actual home, though, two strange things happened. First, he saw his dad's truck in the garage. Usually his dad didn't get home from the office for another couple hours at least. Stepping into the house, Junior opened his mouth to say, "Dad?"

But his father beat him to it. "Junior? Is that you?"

Junior was untying his cleats when he saw his dad's socked feet enter the pantry. "I've never heard you call me Junior," he said.

"Your coach called you that," his dad said. He sounded excited. His socked feet rocked back and forth from heel to toe. "He tried calling here first, but when no one picked up he called me at work."

"Wait," Junior said. "My coach?"

He looked up at his father now and saw that he was grinning. What his dad said next was the second strange thing that happened.

"You made the traveling team!"

TWO

The traveling team's first practice was the very next day. As Junior waited on deck to take some batting practice, he tried to tell himself he was glad he was on the team. Why wouldn't he be?

When he'd arrived at the ball field he'd been given a brand-new uniform. The jersey had "Stallions" stitched across the front of it. The hat had a ferocious-looking horse with steam coming out its nostrils. He was even given a pair of socks with black stirrups painted on them. All his neighborhood team had was T-shirts with their numbers written across them in magic marker.

Junior couldn't even complain about the distance between his house and the ball field. His dad had volunteered to give him a ride.

That wasn't all his dad had volunteered to do, either. He'd also volunteered to be the assistant coach. He was standing in center field right now hitting fly balls to some of Junior's new teammates.

Maybe that's what was bugging him. All the questions he had.

What had gotten into his dad? Since when did he know how to hit fly balls? Junior had been playing baseball every day during the summer for as long as he could remember, and his dad had never hit him fly balls. Why was he so eager to help out now that Junior had made the traveling team?

For that matter, why had Junior made the team at all? The more he thought about it, the more uncertain he was. What he was certain about was that he stunk yesterday. He'd fielded okay, but he hadn't hit a single pitch out of the infield. How could his play yesterday have impressed the coach enough to put him on the team?

The coach, Mr. Grates, was on the mound now, tossing batting practice. He threw one more pitch and barked, "Next batter!"

Junior stepped up to the plate and thought, *Oh, well. I'll earn my spot on the team right now.*

Junior got in his usual straight-legged stance and readied himself to blast the coach's pitch. But when he looked toward the mound he saw that Coach Grates wasn't on it. He was trotting toward the plate. When the coach was a few feet away he said, "I've been meaning to talk to you about your stance, Junior."

Coach Grates was tall enough that Junior had to crane his neck all the way back to look at his face.

"I don't want you to stand straight up like that," Coach Grates continued. "Try bending your knees."

Junior did as he was told.

"Even more," Coach Grates said.

Junior bent his knees even further.

"Even more," Coach Grates said.

By now, Junior was practically as low as the catcher behind the plate. It felt really awkward.

"I don't think I can hit like this," Junior said.

"It's not your job to hit," Coach Grates said. "Let the bigger kids worry about that. It's your job to get on base. And the best way you can do that is by walking. All you have to do is stay there just like that. At your height, most pitchers won't be able to throw it in the strike zone."

Junior watched his coach trot back to the mound. *Just stay there like this?* he thought. What was the fun of batting if you didn't get to hit? His knees already hurt.

Coach Grates kicked his leg up and tossed the ball toward the plate. The pitch was high, just like Junior liked them. He took a step forward with his left foot and slashed at the ball with his bat.

THWACK!

There was that great tingly feeling of hitting a baseball just right. Junior watched the ball zoom through the air and land, finally, just to the right and twenty feet past his dad, who was still hitting fly balls in left field.

"That pitch was high," Coach Grates said. "I don't want you swinging at pitches out of the strike zone."

Had the coach even noticed how far the ball had gone? Junior started to speak, but Coach Grates interrupted him: "Tell you what," he said. "Let's work on your eye at the plate. For the rest of batting practice, don't swing at any of my pitches, okay?"

THREE

Junior was going to quit. If not getting to take any swings during *batting practice* hadn't been bad enough, at the end of practice Coach Grates had gathered the team and gone over hand signals. During the game Coach Grates would stand at third and tell the players what to do with a series of gestures.

If he touched his cap and then his nose, whoever was on first should try to steal. If he touched his cap and then his chin, the batter should try to bunt. If he touched his cap and his right shoulder, the batter should swing away at the next pitch.

"And if I touch my cap and then my left shoulder," Coach Grates had said, "you should keep the bat on your shoulder."

He'd been looking right at Junior as he said it, as if Coach Grates was talking to him and only to him. "In other words, you shouldn't swing no matter what," he said.

Which is why, then and there, Junior decided he was going to quit.

A brand-new uniform wasn't worth an entire summer not getting to hit a baseball. Not even close.

He sat down with the rest of his teammates, crammed his glove and cleats into his baseball bag, and got up to tell Coach Grates he was leaving and he wasn't coming back. But he barely made it three steps before his dad cut him off.

"Hey, buddy!" his dad said. "Was that fun or what?"

Denis was making that big grin again—the same one he'd made when he told Junior about making the team.

"Actually," Junior started to say, but his dad cut him off again.

"How about some ice cream?"

Junior hadn't been out for ice cream with his dad in years.

"Um, sure," he said. "Ice cream would be great."

Still, Junior needed to ask. His father had talked about baseball the whole way to Mega Scoop Ice Cream Parlor. He'd talked about the beauty of baseball fields as they waited in line for their ice cream. He'd talked about getting and breaking in a new glove as they walked outside to sit on Mega Scoop's patio.

So finally, as the two of them sat down at a table, Junior said, "What's gotten into you, Dad?" His dad looked confused, so Junior said, "I mean, I didn't even know you liked baseball."

"I used to," his dad said. "And then I didn't."

Now it was Junior's turn to be confused.

"When I was a kid, my whole life was baseball," his dad explained. His Triple Berry Blast ice cream trickled over a knuckle, and he licked it off. Junior quickly licked his own Chocolate Caramel Craze to stop it from dripping into a puddle forming on the table below.

"I was just like you," his father continued. "When I wasn't playing baseball, I was thinking about it. All fall and winter I'd count down the days until it would be warm enough to play ball again." Some more of his ice cream had melted on his fingers and he licked it off. "The only reason I even played other sports was to distract me until the baseball season started up again."

Junior knew what he meant. That's exactly how he felt about baseball, too. He was pretty sure that's how Swish felt about basketball. He pitched on the neighborhood team, and he was good at it. But he didn't really care one way or the other. He just took the mound because none of his buddies wanted to play basketball.

"Anyway," Junior's dad said, "I was really short like you, too. Too short, as it turned out. When I was about your age I tried out for the traveling team and didn't make it. I tried out the next year, too, and the next one after that, and the next one after that. But eventually I got so discouraged that I quit trying."

His dad stopped talking and once again took a swipe at his ice cream with his tongue.

"But there's lots of short ballplayers," Junior said. "Ivan Rodriguez, Jimmy Rollins, Dustin Pedroia." He could have kept going.

"That's what I thought, too," his dad said. "Too bad the coaches didn't think the same way."

"Is that why you never seemed all that excited about me playing?"

His dad nodded. "I didn't want you to get hurt."

Denis took another lick of his ice cream.

"When your coach called yesterday," he continued, "it was almost like he was telling me *I* had made the team. That sounds kind of weird, doesn't it? But all I'm saying is that I'm so happy for you that it's almost like I'm happy for me. The thought of you getting to wear the nice uniforms, and play in the nice parks, and go on road trips with your teammates—it makes me like baseball all over again."

There was that grin again. Junior's father was smiling so big that he didn't seem to notice the ice cream running down his entire hand.

"Did I answer your question?" he said.

"I think so." Junior pointed at his father's hand and said, "Maybe you should do less question answering and more ice cream eating."

Denis looked at the mess he was making and took a napkin out of the dispenser. "Good point," he said. "Can I ask you a question?"

"Sure, Dad."

"Are you ready for a great season?"

His dad's ice cream was streaming down his fingers too rapidly for the napkin to do much good, but he was still smiling.

"Sure, Dad," Junior said again.

Being on the traveling team couldn't be that bad, could it?

He grabbed a stack of napkins and handed them to his father just as the whole scoop of Triple Berry Blast toppled off the cone.

FOUR

Yeah, maybe it would all be okay. Enough had happened in Junior's life to show him that things sometimes went differently than you wanted them to. But *differently* didn't have to mean *worse*.

Take this game.

It was Junior's first game on the traveling team, and it was scheduled for the same day and time as his neighborhood team's game. He'd had to bring all his neighborhood buddies together and tell them he wouldn't be at their game.

At first he'd dreaded that meeting, but it hadn't turned out that bad. When they found out the reason he was missing the game—he made the traveling team—they were pumped for him.

Way to go! they said.

Congrats! they said.

When's your next game? they asked. *We wanna watch you play!*

And, okay, some of them gave him a hard time.

"What's your jersey size?" one of them asked. "Triple small?"

"Did you have to make an extra hole in your belt to hold up your baseball pants?" another said.

But this was okay, too. Junior knew that the jokes were just that—jokes—and that they were just another way of saying congratulations.

Now that he was at the game, there were other things that didn't go as planned. For one thing, Junior didn't get to play his favorite position, shortstop. Instead, Coach Grates put him at second. But that turned out fine, too. They'd been playing for five innings and he'd already fielded two grounders and turned a double play.

At the plate, well, so far that hadn't been too bad, either. He'd gotten in a crouch just like his coach had taught him, and it had been uncomfortable. But he had to admit that his coach was right: these pitchers couldn't seem to keep their pitches low enough to be called strikes. Unlike the pitchers in the neighborhoods next to his, these guys hadn't grown up pitching to someone so short. He'd been up to bat three times and walked each time.

The batters behind him were good, too. They hit him around the bases twice, which meant he had scored his team's only two runs.

Each time when he got back to the dugout his teammates gave him high fives and slapped him on the back.

His father was the first base coach and shouted, "Way to go!" and "Atta kid, Junior!"

Denis wasn't the only one shouting, either. One cool thing about playing traveling ball was that there were lots of people in the stands. They all clapped like crazy as Junior crossed home plate.

As Junior stood on deck in the bottom of the last inning, he had to admit that traveling ball hadn't been so bad after all.

And the game wasn't over yet.

It was tied 2–2, and they were in the bottom of the last inning, and there weren't any outs.

Jamey, the guy hitting in front of Junior, struck out. Now there was one out.

Junior stepped up to the plate.

He dug his back foot into the dirt, tapped the plate with the end of his bat, and crouched down as low as he could.

The pitcher kicked his leg up and fired a fastball.

As usual, it was way high. Ball one.

The pitcher threw two more high ones before his coach yelled, "Time out!"

The coach headed for the mound and began to chat with his pitcher, so Junior stood up and took a few practice swings in order to stay loose.

"Junior!"

It was Coach Grates calling his name.

Junior looked toward third where his coach was standing. When the two of them were making eye contact, Coach Grates touched his cap and then his left shoulder. Junior understood what the sign meant:

Don't swing. No matter what.

This seemed strange to Junior. He hadn't taken a single swing the whole game. Why was his coach so worried now?

"Batter up!" the ump called.

Junior got in his crouch again, ready for the next pitch. Another fastball, he was guessing. But he was wrong. The pitcher didn't throw a fastball. He didn't throw a curve, either.

Instead, he threw a floater.

He soft-tossed it to the plate. It was batting practice speed, maybe even softer.

Just as Junior was about to swing as hard as he could, though, he remembered his coach's signal and held back.

The ball floated over the plate and into the catcher's glove.

"Strike!" the ump called.

Which was fine by Junior. The fact that the kid threw a strike would encourage him to float it again. And this time, Junior would be ready for it. Maybe this is what Coach Grates had been thinking all along. Maybe he knew that teams would eventually give Junior meatballs like this to crush over the outfielders' heads.

"Junior!"

It was Mr. Grates again. Junior turned toward third and watched his coach once again touch his cap and his left shoulder.

Don't swing. No matter what.

Was he serious? What was Junior supposed to do? Let another one of these meatballs float right on by? He tilted his head at his coach to let him know he was confused. But Coach Grates just did the exact same thing: one touch of the cap, one touch of the left shoulder.

"Step into the batter's box, son," the ump advised Junior.

So Junior did. He stepped into the batter's box. He got into his crouch. And he watched another easy one sail past him. This one was high, just like he liked them.

"Ball four!" the ump called.

Unlike the other times, no one cheered. They were likely as stunned as Junior by what had just happened.

The only one doing any cheering was his dad. When Junior got to first his dad said, "Great patience at the plate, Junior! Way to not get suckered into that nonsense!"

He had his hand extended for a high five.

Nonsense? Junior thought. The only nonsense was letting that pitcher get away with those kinds of pitches. But Junior high-fived his dad, anyway.

"Pay attention to your coach," his dad whispered. "If I were him, I'd tell you to steal. That way you'll be in scoring position for the guys hitting after you."

Junior looked across the diamond at Coach Grates, who was going through a series of signals. None of them meant anything, Junior knew. Coach Grates wasn't asking him to steal second.

But Junior decided to do it, anyway. It was stupid, maybe. But he was angry. And plus, his dad had been right: with one out he wanted to get in scoring position as soon as possible.

Junior took a nice lead off first and waited. Waited for the pitcher to settle himself on the rubber. Waited for him to bring his glove to a set position. Waited for him to start his leg kick.

And then Junior took off for second. He
pumped his arms and watched the base get bigger
as he got closer. He slid feet first and touched
the bag before the catcher's throw made it to the
second baseman.

"Safe!" the umpire screamed.

Now the fans were back into it. They screamed and cheered and clapped as Junior dusted his rear-end and legs off with his hand. It was his first steal of the season—he'd been waiting all offseason for a chance to do it—and he'd forgotten just how good sliding into second could feel.

Two pitches later Delmon, the guy who hit behind him, sent a roller through the infield. Junior read the hit just right and took off for third. As he approached the base he saw Coach Grates waving him around to home.

A few seconds later he was sliding again—only this time it was at home, and it was the game-winning run.

More clapping. More screaming. More whooping with joy. All of it louder this time. Louder by far than any group of people had ever cheered for him. His new teammates were out of the dugout, surrounding him. They were cheering as well.

It was almost enough to forget the frustration he'd experienced earlier.

Eventually, the crowd and players turned their attention to Delmon, the kid who had the game-winning hit. Junior was turning to do the same when a hand grasped his shoulder and turned him the other way.

It was Coach Grates. They were close enough that Junior once again had to crane his neck to see the man's face. His coach was still gripping Junior's shoulder tightly.

And he wasn't smiling.

"I didn't tell you to steal second," he said. His voice was so even it was scary. All of this loud, happy noise around them, but Coach Grates spoke in a completely regular voice.

"I—I—" Junior stammered, "it's just—"

"It's my fault, Coach," someone said.

It was Junior's dad. He placed his hand on Junior's other shoulder.

"I think I confused him," he said. "I mentioned it might be a good situation to steal, and, well, like I said, it's my fault."

Finally, Coach Grates released his hand from Junior's shoulder. "Just so long as it doesn't happen again," he said.

He turned and walked toward first, where everyone else was crowding around Delmon.

On the truck ride home, Junior's dad was saying something about the game when Junior interrupted him: "I wasn't confused," Junior said.

"What?"

"I wasn't confused. By you or by Coach Grates's signals. I knew he didn't want me to steal, but I did it anyway."

"Why?"

"Because you were right," Junior said. "I needed to get into scoring position."

His dad started to say something but again Junior interrupted him. "And because he told me not to swing when that kid started floating the ball to me. It was stupid."

His dad sighed. "First of all, you shouldn't talk about your coach that way. And second, it wasn't stupid."

"Yes it was."

"You had three balls on you. It was the right decision to tell you not to swing."

"Maybe the first time," Junior said. "But the second time I had a strike against me. It was a hitter's count. I could've smoked that pitch."

"The next pitch was a ball."

"He didn't know it was going to be."

"Look, Junior, you're not going to like everything your coach has you do. But he knows what he's doing. I think he played some college ball." They were turning into their driveway now. His dad reached for the garage door opener. "Besides," he said as the garage door lifted, "you should be glad you have a role on the team. That's what's most important."

"I could have smoked that pitch," Junior said again, because he got the impression his dad didn't believe him.

FIVE

By the last inning of the next game, Junior had to keep reminding himself to pay attention. His dad had been right, he tried to tell himself. He was lucky just to have a spot on the team. Lots of kids, including some from his neighborhood team, would have loved to get to play on this team.

Except that was the problem: he wasn't really getting to play. Yeah, he got to play the field, and that was great. He'd been a part of another double play just an inning ago. But he didn't get to bat. At least not really. He got to stand at the plate and watch the ball go by.

Maybe the last team's coach had talked to this team's coach. However it had happened, word had gotten out: no matter how slow you throw it, the teeny-tiny kid isn't going to swing.

By now, Junior knew the routine. He'd step up to the plate, his coach would holler his name, and then he'd get the sign not to swing. No matter what.

After the pitch, they'd go through the same thing all over again.

It was humiliating: all these people—players, fans, coaches—watching him just stand there as the ball dropped gently into the catcher's glove. (No, he didn't stand there. He crouched—almost like he was afraid, like he was cowering from the ball.)

It was frustrating. What Junior liked to do more than anything in the world was feel that tingling up his arms as his bat made perfect contact with a pitch, but he might as well not have even brought a bat with him.

Mostly, it wasn't fun. Junior felt whiny admitting this to himself. After all, he had the opportunity to wear a great uniform while playing the best game ever invented.

Except, of course, he wasn't actually getting to play the best game ever invented. Not really. Not completely.

And, to make matters worse, his other team, his neighborhood team, had a game today as well.

So while Junior crouched there watching meatball after meatball plop into the mitt behind him, he knew he could have been standing tall with Swish and his friends taking mighty whacks at flaming fastballs.

To make matters even worse than that, Coach Grates' strategy was working. Sort of. At least according to his dad. He'd been up three times and been walked twice. The other time he struck out without ever taking the bat off his shoulder.

Still, when he got to first base, his dad told him that he was doing great. "You're doing your job," he said. "You're getting on base more times than you're getting out."

His job. If you wanted to look at it like that, Junior supposed, his dad was right. But he didn't want to look at baseball as a job. He wanted to play baseball like it was a game. Because it was a game, wasn't it?

Wasn't it supposed to be fun?

That's what the others on this team got to have. Fun. They got to swing whenever they wanted to. And that's what he would be having if he was playing on his neighborhood team. But instead he was here, and once again it was the last inning, and he wasn't allowed to swing.

This time, they were down a run, 5–4. There were two outs. But it felt pretty much the same: here was Junior, up to bat, squatting almost as low as the catcher, trying to convince himself to pay attention.

That's when he realized he didn't have to pay attention. Not while he was batting. All he had to do was stay in this ridiculous stance until the ump said, "Strike three, you're out!" or "Ball four, take your base."

And it was this realization that really made him angry. He didn't have to pay attention. While playing *baseball*. It was ridiculous. It was dumb. It was stupid. This coach—he was stupid. Junior felt like screaming it: "The coach is STUPID!"

If he did, he knew his dad would scold him for talking that way about a coach, and in a way his dad would be right. As a rule, players shouldn't call their coach stupid. But this wasn't just any other coach. Coach Grates was trying to ruin the sport for Junior!

As Junior thought about his stupid coach, the pitcher must have thrown a pitch, because the ump yelled, "Strike!"

Yep, Junior thought. *Stupid. My coach is stupid.* Stupid because he'd taken a game and made it un-fun. Stupid because he'd taken a game and made it a job.

Mostly, though, this coach was stupid because he'd taken baseball and made it so you didn't have to pay attention. Which, Junior now understood, completely defeated the purpose of playing baseball. It was supposed to be a game where you had to pay attention at all times. That's what people who didn't like baseball didn't understand.

The pitcher must have thrown another pitch to Junior, because the ump called, "Strike!"

Junior could hear Swish making all those complaints. "It doesn't have as much action as basketball," he liked to say. "It gets boring between pitches."

What Swish didn't understand was that baseball required your attention constantly. Things changed between pitches. Fielders moved in or out and side to side. Batters changed their strategy. Coaches helped them do it.

Except for this coach. He didn't change his strategy. Not ever. And what was the fun of that?

So this time Junior decided to change it for him. He decided to pay attention again. The pitcher lobbed another one over the plate, and Junior took a gigantic swing at it.

CRACK!

The ball moved so fast it almost sizzled through the air. It went long and deep, and it went foul.

The fans cheered. "Way to go, Junior!" they screamed. "Hit another one like that!"

But they weren't the only ones who were screaming. For the first time, Coach Grates was screaming, too.

"Junior! I told you not to swing! You hear me?"

The anger in his voice silenced the crowd.

Not to swing? they seemed to be thinking. *Why wouldn't you want him to swing?*

My thoughts exactly, Junior thought.

But instead he said, "You got it, Coach."

And the pitcher tossed the ball over the plate,
and the umpire said, "Strike three—game over!"
And Junior dropped the bat and started running.

Over his shoulder, he heard his dad yell,
"Junior, where are you going?"

And Junior thought: Home. I have to get home.

SIX

He kept saying it to himself as he ran.

"Home. I have to get home."

He said it between breaths, between the clicks of his cleats against the road.

He ran, and then he jogged, and then, when he could hardly breathe any more, he walked as quickly as he could. "Home," he said to himself. "I have to get home."

He was in such a hurry to get there that he didn't realize until he arrived that he'd left out a word.

He wasn't going home. He was going to home *plate*. *His* home base.

He was going to his home field—the one in his neighborhood, the one that he'd been playing on since he was five years old.

And now he was there. He was here. He was home.

His whole team saw him coming. Or they heard him coming, anyway. Heard his breathing, heard his cleats.

"Junior!"

"Hey, man!"

"Looking sharp, Junior!"

He'd forgotten he was still wearing his traveling uniform. What he wouldn't give to be wearing a T-shirt jersey just like all his former teammates had on. He was next to his old ball field, looking out at his former teammates.

Standing out here and wearing this uniform, he felt like an outsider at his own field. Then he heard swishing.

"You're just in time, Junior."

He turned toward the field. Swish was coming

toward him.

"I was afraid I'd be too late," Junior said.

"Nope," Swish said. "I was just about to bat." Swish reached out and handed his bat and jersey to Junior. "Here. Take it. Pinch hit for me."

"You sure?"

"Sure I'm sure. Come in here and show these guys what's what. This game is boring anyway." Swish smiled. "That way I can go shoot some hoops."

Now they were both smiling.

"If you say so," Junior said.

"Are we going to play or what?" someone from the other team said.

So Junior stepped to the plate. This time, he stood up straight and tall as he waited for the pitch—or as tall as he could possibly make himself.

Unlike the traveling game, this game didn't only last six innings. It went on as long as everyone wanted to keep playing. At some point, when some players said they had to go home, someone else announced, "Last inning!" and they all agreed that it was.

No one had remembered to officially keep score, and both teams claimed that they had won. Junior joined in on the debate, but he hadn't been there for most of it. And even if he had, he wouldn't have really cared one way or the other.

The late-game base running heroics of that first traveling game had been fun, but he didn't really miss them—not today he didn't. Nor did he miss the crowd. He'd always wanted to play in front of a crowd, but it wasn't really the reason he played baseball. He understood that now better than ever. In fact, right now he cared so little about who was watching him that he didn't notice his father until one of his teammates pointed him out.

His dad was standing behind the backstop, leaning against his truck.

"Sorry I ran off like that," Junior said.

His dad nodded. He jerked his thumb at the truck. "Your grandmother always laughed at me for buying this truck," he said.

Junior had no idea what to say to that.

"She said I was too small to be driving around in a truck," his dad continued. "She didn't really mean that there should be a height requirement for trucks. A truck isn't a ride at an amusement park. She just knew me well enough to know why I drove a truck."

He looked at Junior but didn't seem to be waiting for him to speak.

"To prove something. That's why I bought it. I was a tiny little businessman and I wanted to fit in—don't ask me with who because I don't know. Now I go to work and can hardly fit in the parking lot and have to jump in and out of my own vehicle. Do you see my point?"

"Don't buy trucks?" Junior said.

His dad laughed. "No. Just don't buy a truck for the wrong reasons. Your grandma was even shorter than me, but she knew who she was, and if she'd had a truck it would have fit her just fine."

"Okay."

"What I'm trying to say is that I think you're like her. You fit in . . . with yourself. I'm not being very clear, am I?"

"Not really," Junior said.

"What I'm trying to say is that I drove here angry and ready to holler, and then I saw you play. And you're good, Junior. You're really, really good."

This compliment was as unexpected as the lecture on trucks.

"And I'm really sorry I never understood that until right now."

Junior didn't know what to say other than, "It's okay."

His father shook his head. "No it isn't. As far as I'm concerned, this field is where you should be. And I think you knew that all along, didn't you?"

"Yeah."

"So why'd you keep playing for that team? As a favor to me?"

Junior nodded his head.

"In that case, I'm going to ask you to do me one more favor, okay?"

"What?"

"Let's talk to your coach about letting you hit."

Before Junior could answer a voice interrupted him from behind.

"You don't have to."

Shocked, Junior turned around to see Coach Grates.

SEVEN

It turned out Coach Grates had driven by the sandlot field on his way home from the Stallions' last game. And as he did, Coach Grates saw Junior smacking the ball to all corners of the field.

"Maybe we should let you swing away in the next game," he had told Junior and his dad in the parking lot of the sandlot field.

So far, the Stallions' next game had gone similarly to the first two. Both teams managed to get a few runs across the plate. They headed into the seventh inning tied 3–3. And Junior was no longer forced to crouch low for his at-bats.

But there was one problem. And it was a big problem. Junior stood up tall in his first at-bat and popped out to the pitcher on the first pitch. Then he struck out on three pitches in the third inning. Coach Grates had patted him on the back after that. But Junior could just sense what was coming. In his next at-bat, he just knew he would be crouching again.

It felt like the whole world was watching as Junior walked to the plate in the top of the fifth. The Stallions were playing Kirkwood, the next town to the west and big rivals. And Alex O'Neil was on the mound for Kirkwood. Everybody knew he had the fastest fastball in the league.

Maybe it was a good idea to crouch, Junior thought as he adjusted his batting gloves. After all,

Jamey was on first base for the Stallions. If Junior walked it would put Jamey on second base—in scoring position.

Junior stepped into the batter's box and tapped home plate once with his bat. Then he looked over to third base, waiting for Coach Grates to tap his cap and left shoulder—don't swing no matter what. Indeed Coach Grates tapped his cap. But then he tapped his right shoulder. Swing away!

Junior couldn't believe it. He looked over at his dad, standing behind first base, who nodded in approval. So Junior dug his feet into the dirt and stood just as tall as he would if Swish were pitching.

THWACK!

Junior sent the first pitch sailing toward the gap in left-center. It landed between the two outfielders and rolled all the way to the fence. By the time Kirkwood had gotten the ball back to the infield Junior was standing on second and Jamey had scored the go-ahead run.

"Way to go, Junior!" he heard his dad call out from first.

"Nice swing!" somebody yelled from the stands.

The crowd was going wild, but Junior could hardly hear them. For a moment he felt almost like he did when he was playing on his home field. Suddenly baseball felt fun again! But before Junior knew it, Vince had hit another single and Junior was booking toward third.

"Nice hit," Coach Grates said, patting Junior on the back once he got there. "Maybe if you stick around we can do that more often—make this team as fun as your sandlot team."

THE END